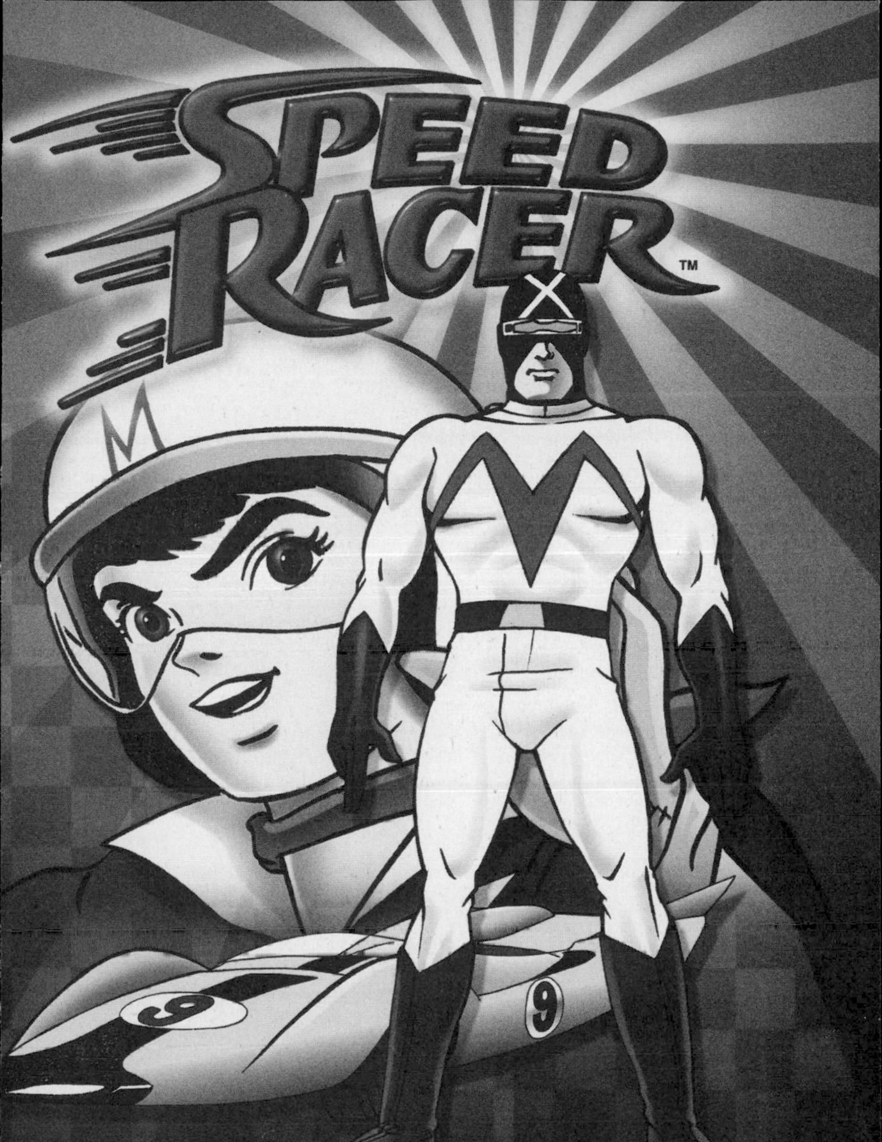

Challenge of the Masked Racer

GROSSET & DUNLAP
Published by the Penguin Group
Penguin Group (USA) Inc., 375 Hudson Street,
New York, New York 10014, USA
Penguin Group (Canada), 90 Eglinton Avenue East, Suite 700,
Toronto, Ontario M4P 2Y3, Canada
(a division of Pearson Penguin Canada Inc.)
Penguin Books Ltd., 80 Strand, London WC2R 0RL, England
Penguin Group Ireland, 25 St. Stephen's Green,
Dublin 2, Ireland
(a division of Penguin Books Ltd.)
Penguin Group (Australia), 250 Camberwell Road,
Camberwell, Victoria 3124, Australia
(a division of Pearson Australia Group Pty. Ltd.)
Penguin Books India Pvt. Ltd., 11 Community Centre,
Panchsheel Park, New Delhi—110 017, India
Penguin Group (NZ), 67 Apollo Drive,
Rosedale, North Shore 0632, New Zealand
(a division of Pearson New Zealand Ltd.)
Penguin Books (South Africa) (Pty.) Ltd., 24 Sturdee Avenue,
Rosebank, Johannesburg 2196, South Africa

Penguin Books Ltd., Registered Offices: 80 Strand, London WC2R 0RL, England

The publisher does not have any control over and does not assume any responsibility for author
or third-party websites or their content.

The scanning, uploading, and distribution of this book via the Internet or via any other means
without the permission of the publisher is illegal and punishable by law. Please purchase only
authorized electronic editions, and do not participate in or encourage electronic piracy of copy-
righted materials. Your support of the author's rights is appreciated.

www.speedracer.com

Library of Congress Cataloging-in-Publication Data is available.

ISBN 978-0-448-44805-3   10 9 8 7 6 5 4 3 2 1

Challenge of the Masked Racer

by Chase Wheeler

Grosset & Dunlap

The Marvels of the Mach 5

The Mach 5 is one of the most
powerful and amazing racing cars in
the world. Pops Racer designed the Mach 5
with features you won't see on any other car.
All of the features can be controlled by
buttons on the steering wheel.

 This button releases powerful jacks to boost the car so Sparky, the mechanic, can quickly make any necessary repairs or adjustments.

 Press this button and the Mach 5 sprouts special grip tires for traction over any terrain. At the same time, an incredible 5,000 torque of horsepower is distributed equally to each wheel by auxiliary engines.

 For use when Speed Racer has to race over heavily wooded terrain, powerful rotary saws protrude from the front of the Mach 5 to slash and cut any and all obstacles.

 Pressing the D button releases a powerful deflector that seals the cockpit into an air-conditioned, crash and bulletproof, watertight chamber. Inside it, Speed Racer is completely isolated and shielded.

 The button for special illumination allows Speed Racer to see much farther and more clearly than with ordinary headlights. It's invaluable in some of the weird and dangerous places he races the Mach 5.

 Press this button when the Mach 5 is underwater. First the cockpit is supplied with oxygen, then a periscope is raised to scan the surface of the water. Everything that is seen is relayed down to the cockpit by television.

 This releases a homing robot from the front of the car. The homing robot can carry pictures or tape-recorded messages to anyone or anywhere Speed Racer wants.

Speed Racer stepped on the gas of the Mach 5. The sleek white race car expertly handled the curves of the winding road.

Speed wasn't in a race. It was a bright, sunny day, and he and his girlfriend, Trixie, were headed for the beach. A mermaid doll dangled from the Mach 5's rearview mirror. A flock of seagulls cried out as they flew overhead. A salty breeze rippled through Trixie's bouncy brown hair.

"There's the ocean up ahead, Speed," Trixie remarked. The bright blue water came into view over the railing.

Speed handled another curve in the road. Now they were driving alongside the ocean. Waves lapped up against the cliff that separated the ocean from the road. The seagulls flew alongside Speed as he sped down the road, almost as though they were racing the Mach 5.

Suddenly, a black-and-white dog appeared on the road in front of the car. Speed and Trixie gasped.

Speed reacted quickly. He pressed the A button on the Mach 5's steering wheel. Hydraulic jacks emerged from under the body of the car. They propelled the Mach 5 straight up into the air. The race car hopped over the little dog.

Speed and Trixie smiled at each other. Speed's dad, Pops Racer, had engineered the Mach 5. Pops had outfitted the car with extra features to help the Mach 5 on the world's most dangerous racecourses. But the features came in handy off the racetrack, too.

They left the dog safely behind them and continued on down the road. But as they neared the docks, something made Speed slow down.

A huge steamer ship was anchored at one of the docks. A crowd was gathered in front of the ship. They were looking at a race car being lowered from the ship with chains.

The yellow car had a black number 9 on the side. Two yellow fins stuck out of the car's rear body. A black stripe ran from the windshield down

to the front of the car, ending in a wicked-looking sharp nose.

A man in a white racing suit waited on the dock for the car to be lowered. He wore a black mask over his head that covered his eyes and chin. Only his nose and mouth were exposed. This was the infamous Racer X.

Speed parked the Mach 5 and he and Trixie got out to watch. The people in the crowd wore suits. They carried microphones, cameras, and notebooks. Speed guessed they were news reporters.

"Racer X's car is being unloaded from the ship!" one reporter cried out. He wore glasses, and a pink suit with a blue tie.

Next to him, a photographer holding a camera nodded. "This means there will be trouble in the race."

"Every time that masked racer has been in a race, there have been mysterious crashes," the reporter said.

"Rumor has it that Racer X is causing the cars to crash," the photographer added.

A woman reporter frowned behind them. "Nobody's been able to prove that," she pointed out.

The reporter grinned. "Why do you think I'm here? I want to catch him in the act! I'm going to keep a close eye on Racer X."

The yellow race car safely landed on the dock. Racer X unhooked the chains that had lowered the car from the boat. He began to check the car's tires. He kept his back to the reporters, ignoring them.

Speed and Trixie watched. Racer X was famous in the racing world. They had never been so close to a celebrity before!

Trixie had a dreamy look in her dark eyes. "He looks mysterious in that mask," she said. "Handsome, too."

Speed admired the masked racer for another reason. "He drives faster than a rocket, and he won the Grand Prix at Le Mans four years in a row," he told Trixie. "He's won just about every race he's ever entered."

"No kidding!" Trixie remarked.

"He's raced against some of the top racers in

the world, and he's beaten all of them," Speed said. His blue eyes shone with admiration as he talked about Racer X.

Trixie sighed. "I hope I get to see what he really looks like."

Speed chuckled. "Sorry, but nobody's ever seen him. They don't even know his real name, or where he's from. That's why they call him Racer X."

"Masked Racer, who do you think will win the Trans-Country Race?" one reporter asked as he approached Racer X.

Racer X didn't answer. He kept working on his car.

"Do you think any cars will crash in the race?" another reporter asked.

Racer X turned and silently scowled at the reporter. The man grinned. "Aha! So you're keeping *that* a secret."

Racer X ignored the question. He jumped into the driver's seat of his car. Photographers began snapping pictures like crazy.

"Hold it, Masked Racer! Let me get another shot," a photographer called out.

But Racer X just revved the engine. A short

man with a bow tie, mustache, and balding head pushed his way through the crowd.

"Racer X, my name is Mr. Wiley," he said. "I'm on the committee of the Trans-Country Race. I'd like to talk to you for a few minutes."

Racer X drove off without a word. Mr. Wiley's face turned red with anger as he watched the Masked Racer go.

"Hey, don't go! We've got more questions!" a reporter cried.

The Masked Racer drove past Speed and Trixie. His race car screeched to a halt. He looked at the two of them in his rearview mirror. Then he drove off once again.

"Oooh!" Trixie swooned. They'd almost had a close encounter with Racer X!

But Speed frowned.

That Masked Racer sure is strange, he thought.

Then he smiled at Trixie.

"Come on," he said. "We've got to catch some waves!"

Back at Speed's house, Pops Racer sat behind his desk. Speed's little brother, Spritle, sat at a nearby table. His pet chimpanzee, Chim Chim, sat next to him. They were happily eating oranges.

Pops didn't look happy at all. He frowned under his black mustache as he looked at the two men in front of him.

One man was tall and thin, with a small mustache under his long nose. He wore a green suit, a matching hat, and glasses. The other man was short and round with slicked-back black hair. He wore a maroon suit and a green bow tie.

The thin man slapped a pile of money on the desk.

"A thousand bucks. What do you say?" he asked.

Pops folded his muscular arms across his desk.

"Hmmm," he replied as he closed his eyes.

Spritle's brown eyes grew wide. He looked at Chim Chim. "A thousand bucks! We could buy a lot of candy with that!"

Chim Chim jumped up and down in his seat. *"Eek! Eek!"* he agreed.

Pops still didn't answer.

"My Alpha Team has got to win the great Trans-Country Race," the thin man explained. "With the Masked Racer in the race, my team won't have a chance. You've got to let your son Speed Racer join my boys. With him on our side, we'll be able to beat that Racer X."

"Hmmm," Pops said again. He didn't seem to be impressed.

The thin man slapped another pile of money on the table. "I'll increase my offer. How does two thousand bucks sound?"

Spritle's eyes nearly popped out of his head. "Wow!" he cried.

Chim Chim tried to count to two thousand on his fingers. He didn't get very far. He took off his red shoes and tried counting on his toes. That didn't work, either.

"Eek!" Chim Chim cried. Then he fainted. The

thought of all that money was too much for him.

It still didn't impress Pops. He kept his eyes closed and his arms folded.

The thin man was starting to sweat. "How about it? Will you let Speed Racer join the Alpha Team for two thousand?"

Pops still didn't answer.

The fat man in the maroon suit started laughing. The thin man stomped up to him.

"What's so funny?" he demanded.

"I'm laughing because you're offering a measly two thousand bucks to Mr. Racer," he explained. "But I'll pay three thousand for Speed to be on my team!"

Pops thoughtfully stroked his chin. Things were starting to get interesting now.

"How about it, Mr. Racer?" the fat man asked. He opened a briefcase and took out a big pile of money. He put it on the table next to the pile that was already there. "Here's the money. I'll even throw in an extra fifty cents."

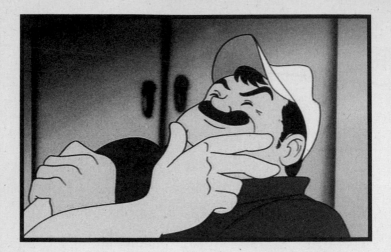

The coins clattered on the table. Pops opened his eyes.

Now it was the thin man's turn to laugh. "Only three thousand? I'll make it four." He smacked more money down. "How about it, Mr. Racer?"

Pops shook his head no.

Sprite and Chim Chim watched with glee.

"Oh boy, the price is getting better and better!" Spritle said. "I hope it keeps going up."

The fat man looked serious now. "I'm willing to make it five thousand dollars and fifty cents."

"Keep holding out, Pops!" Spritle cheered. "Maybe they'll go up to a million!"

But Pops had had enough.

"Keep the money!" Pops barked. "Speed won't be on either one of your teams!"

Pops was a big man with a barrel chest and arms muscled from his years working as a pro wrestler. When Pops was angry, he could frighten a bear. The two moneymen were no different. The frightened men grabbed their cash and ran out. Spritle frowned.

"Too bad. Now we won't be able to buy any candy!" he complained.

Pops let out a sigh. Speed was a good driver. But he wasn't ready to go pro yet. And no amount of money was going to change Pops's mind!

●　　●　　●　　●

The sun set over the harbor, casting shades of gold and red over the water. Speed and Trixie sat on the hood of the Mach 5 and watched the beautiful sight. They'd had a great day at the beach, but meeting Racer X had definitely been the most exciting part of their day.

"Racer X will probably win the Trans-Country Race, won't he, Speed?" Trixie asked.

"I guess so," Speed answered.

Trixie glanced at Speed. "But he doesn't *have* to win, does he?"

"What are you hinting at?" Speed asked.

"You should enter the race!" Trixie urged. "I'm sure you're the only one who can beat Racer X."

Speed sighed. "Maybe I am, but maybe I'm

not." He looked out at the waves, and a sad look crossed his face. "We'll never know because I'm not racing."

"Oh, come on, Speed," Trixie teased. "Won't you do it for me?"

"You know I can't, Trixie," Speed replied. "It'll make Pops super angry."

Trixie grinned. "If I know him, he'll calm down once he sees you're going to win."

Speed and Trixie laughed. That sounded like Pops, all right.

A red race car pulled up next to the Mach 5. The driver wore a red racing suit and a red helmet with a white arrow on it. Speed recognized Zoomer Slick, a young driver on the racing circuit.

"Hey, Speed," Slick greeted him. "Guess who you're looking at? The winner of the Trans-Country Race, that's who!"

Trixie looked at Speed and rolled her eyes.

"I just signed up with Mr. Fixer for the Alpha Team," Slick went on. "Our team's got lots of

spirit. One of us is going to beat the Masked Racer, and that's going to be me! Too bad your father didn't take all that money Mr. Fixer offered him. Otherwise you'd be driving for the Alpha Team instead of me."

Speed and Trixie looked at each other. Had Pops really turned down a chance for Speed to enter the race?

Slick grinned. He wanted to get under Speed's skin, and he'd succeeded. "See you after I win!" he called out. Then he waved and zoomed away.

"Good luck, Slick!" Speed called after him, and he meant it. Slick might not be the nicest guy, but he was a fellow driver, and Speed was a good sport.

Trixie scowled. "He's so conceited! Now you have to enter that race, Speed. You have to beat Slick *and* the Masked Racer!"

Speed watched Slick drive off down the road. Trixie was making sense. Speed knew he was a better racer than Slick. So why did Slick get to race, while Speed sat on the sidelines? It wasn't fair.

"Let's go, Trixie," Speed said, jumping into the Mach 5.

"Where are we going?" Trixie asked.

Speed grinned. "You'll see."

The Racer family gathered around the television that night. Pops wore a bathrobe and sat in his favorite armchair. Speed and his mom sat in chairs on either side of Pops. Mom Racer was a pretty woman with brown hair and a friendly smile. Her hands moved quickly as she knitted a blanket. Spritle and Chim Chim sat at a table, snacking on donuts.

A news announcer's voice blared from the TV set.

"And now from the world of sports," he said. "The Trans-Country auto race will start in two days. The race is one of the most grueling and dangerous in the world. Drivers will race on a 300-mile course. Some of the top champions in the sport of motor racing will be participating."

Race cars zoomed across the TV screen. Spritle

watched with wide eyes. Even though he wasn't old enough to race yet, he loved everything about racing. He was a Racer, after all.

Chim Chim thought of a way to trick Spritle. He picked up the last donut on the plate. Then he put the ball of yarn that Mom was using on the plate. The chimpanzee giggled, waiting to see what would happen.

The picture on the screen changed to show a group of drivers in red racing uniforms. Zoomer Slick stood in front of them.

"Let me introduce a few of the most famous drivers to our viewing audience," the announcer went on. "Zoomer Slick is the top driver for the Alpha Team."

"He's in the race?" Spritle asked. He grabbed the ball of yarn from the plate. Then he bit into it, thinking it was a donut.

"Ha! Ha!" Chim Chim laughed.

Now a picture of the Masked Racer appeared on the screen.

"This is Racer X, known throughout the world as the Masked Racer," the announcer said. "He has been known to bring back luck to many races."

Pops nodded. "That may be true, but he's one of the best racers I've ever seen!"

The announcer wasn't finished.

"In addition to the Masked Racer, one of the top contenders and last-minute entries is a newcomer, Speed Racer," he said.

Mom Racer gasped. She leaned forward, pulling the ball of yarn with her. Poor Spritle was still holding on to it, and he tumbled off of his chair.

Speed braced himself. Pops was definitely not going to be happy about this—and when Pops wasn't happy, *nobody* was happy.

"Speed has raced in very few meets so far," the announcer went on. "He will enter this race driving the Mach 5, a special racing car designed by his father, Pops Racer."

Pops's face turned as red as an Alpha Team uniform. Mom Racer grinned.

"The race is expected to be a close competition between Speed Racer and the Masked Racer," the announcer finished.

Pops exploded. "You're not supposed to be in that race!" he yelled.

Spritle frowned. "Here we go again. Pops is blowing another gasket!"

Pops got out of his chair. The big man looked like an angry volcano about to blow.

"Speed, I don't want you in that race!" Pops

fumed. "Under no circumstances are you allowed to enter. Understand?"

Mom Racer stepped up behind Pops and put a hand on his shoulder. "Now, dear, calm down," she said firmly.

Spritle smiled. "Here we go. Pops will change his mind."

Pops softened. "I'm only trying to do what's best for you, son," he told Speed. "You don't have enough skill and experience yet to race against the Masked Racer. It requires advanced technical skills. Sharp reflexes are necessary over every inch of that racing course."

Speed looked down at the floor. He had heard

this from Pops many times. Speed had trained hard to be a racer. But it seemed Pops would never be convinced that Speed was ready to race.

"Let me tell you about your older brother, Rex," Pops said, his voice softening. "Rex left home many years ago. He and I had a bad argument. It all started when he was eighteen years old, the same age you are now."

Speed looked at the photo of Rex that hung on the wall. His brother sat in a yellow race car, a look of determination on his face.

Pops continued his story. "Rex joined a race without asking my permission," he said. "He used a car I spent years building . . ."

Pops got a faraway look on his face as he remembered that day. Pops had arrived at the racetrack as fast as he could. Rex was speeding around the track. Two cars crashed in front of him, leaving Rex in first place. But Rex was reckless. His car spun out of control and crashed into the barrier wall.

 31

Pops had rushed to the car. Rex climbed out. Thankfully, he didn't have a scratch on him.

That's when the argument began. Pops remembered it like it was yesterday.

"I'm sorry, Pops," Rex had said. *"A few yards farther and I would have been the winner. I did such a great job of driving, I deserved to win the race."*

"You deserved to lose!" Pops cried angrily. *"Your driving was terrible."*

"What do you mean, terrible? I would have won if my car hadn't gone into a spin," Rex said, getting angry himself.

"Right," Pops said. "And if you had more experience, that wouldn't have happened."

"It was just an accident, Pops!" Rex protested.

"I don't care," Pops shot back. "I don't want to find you behind the wheel of a car again. And that's final!"

Rex's eyes blazed with anger and pride. "Then I'll have to become a champion without you, Pops. I'm leaving home."

Rex turned and walked down the track, leaving Pops and the burning car behind him.

That was the last time anyone in the Racer

family had seen Rex Racer. Pops's eyes filled and began to tear at the memory. He looked at Speed.

"That's why I want you to get more experience, Speed," Pops said. "I don't want you to crash like Rex did. Your brother could have been really hurt."

Spritle stepped up between them.

"But Pops, don't you know Speed is the best racing car driver in the world?" he piped up.

"I didn't ask you, Spritle!" Pops bellowed.

Chim Chim hid behind Spritle's back, shivering.

Mom Racer looked up from her knitting. "It's getting pretty late. It's time for bed, boys. Good night, Spritle. Good night, Speed."

"Good night!" Spritle and Speed said together.

Minutes later, Speed was in bed, reading the latest issue of his favorite racing magazine. But he couldn't concentrate. He set the magazine on his chest and looked up at the ceiling.

Oh, Rex, where are you? Speed thought. He turned over and pounded his fist on his pillow. *Why don't you come home again, where you belong? Mom and Pops miss you. I miss you, too. I'm going to race against the Masked Racer whether Pops likes it or not. I wish you could be here to see me. I've got to beat him, I've got to! If I beat the Masked Racer, Pops will know I'm ready to go pro.*

Speed rolled over and fell into a fitful sleep.

The next morning, a group of men met in a hotel room.

One of the men was Mr. Wiley, the man who had talked to Racer X on the docks. It's true that he was on the committee of the Trans-Country Race. But that's not all. He secretly managed the Alpha Team racers as well. Wiley sat in a fancy leather chair.

Standing next to Wiley was a tall, thin man with a mustache. Mr. Fixer was the man who had offered Pops thousands of dollars to get Speed Racer on the Alpha Team.

Zoomer Slick and the other Alpha Team racer stood in front of Wiley and Fixer. Wiley had called this secret meeting to talk about the Trans-Country Race.

"I want my team to win the Trans-Country

Race no matter what the price," Wiley said. His beady brown eyes focused on Slick. "Do you understand, Slick?"

"You can count on me, Mr. Wiley," Slick said confidently. "It doesn't matter if the Masked Racer and Speed Racer are in the race. I'm going to beat them both."

"Smart boy," Mr. Wiley replied. "But I heard that the Masked Racer is pretty tricky."

"No matter what trick he pulls, I'll be pulling it first," Slick said. "Don't worry. I'll beat him."

Mr. Wiley laughed. "That's the dirty fighting spirit!"

Slick leaned closer to Mr. Wiley. "When I do win, I'll expect to be paid a lot of money."

Mr. Wiley smiled. "I promise, Slick. You'll get everything you deserve."

Mr. Fixer stepped between them.

"Hey, Mr. Wiley, I just found out that the Masked Racer is staying at a house in town," he said, his voice high with excitement. "I'll bet he's making plans to beat us."

Mr. Wiley shrugged. "So?"

"So we'd better make some plans to beat him!" Mr. Fixer pointed out.

"Don't worry," Slick bragged. "When I'm out on that track I'll do my stuff. He won't know what hit him."

Mr. Wiley nodded approvingly. Slick was just the man he needed on his team.

"Good luck, Slick!"

Over at the Racer house, Spritle and Chim Chim were playing outside in the backyard. They had two toy race cars. One looked exactly like the Mach 5. The other was a yellow car with a number 9 on the side—just like Racer X had.

The motorized cars zoomed around a racecourse Spritle had made in a big, long sandbox. The two cars were side by side.

Spritle narrated the race. "Number 9, driven by the Masked Racer, is beating Speed Racer, driving the Mach 5. Now they are neck and neck and the Masked Racer is trying to make Speed crash!"

Both cars sped to the end of the sandbox. They flew over the edge and landed nosedown in a pile of dirt.

"They both crash!" Spritle cried.

Spritle reached out to pick up the cars. Then he stopped.

The cars had crashed at the feet of a man in a white racing uniform. The man wore a black mask over his face.

"The Masked Racer!" Spritle screamed. "Hide!"

Spritle and Chim Chim tripped over each other, trying to get away. Spritle picked himself up, ran, and then crashed into a chair swing!

"Don't be afraid," Racer X said.

"I'm not." Spritle sat in the chair and tried to look tough.

"Isn't your name Spritle?" Racer X asked.

Spritle jumped off of the swing and waved his right fist at Racer X. "That's what it is, and I'm stronger than I look. So watch out!"

The Masked Racer smiled. "I will, Spritle."

"What did you come here for?" Spritle asked suspiciously.

"To ask you to do something for me," he replied. He held out a white envelope. "I want you to give this letter to your brother Speed."

"I don't get it," Spritle said. "Why don't you give it to him yourself?"

"I don't want anyone to know about it," the

Masked Racer answered mysteriously. "Please take it."

Racer X tucked the letter inside the front pocket of Spritle's overalls. Then he gave Spritle a gentle pat on the head. "Now be a good boy, Spritle," he said kindly. Then he jumped in his car and drove off.

Spritle watched him go. "Come on, Chim Chim. We have to give this letter to Speed!"

They raced around the house to the garage. Speed was outside, washing the Mach 5. Spritle took the letter out of his pocket and began to wave it.

"Speed! Speed! Look! The Masked Racer gave me a letter to give to you!" he cried.

Speed turned off the hose. "The Masked Racer? Really?"

He took the letter from his little brother. Spritle grinned, proud that he had been given such an important task.

Speed opened the envelope and read the letter. He frowned.

"What does it say, Speed?" Spritle asked, jumping up and down with excitement.

"It doesn't have anything to do with you, Spritle," Speed said. "It's between me and the Masked Racer. Promise you won't tell anyone?"

Spritle nodded. "Okay."

That night, Speed had trouble sleeping once again. He kept thinking about the letter from the Masked Racer—and the big Trans-Country Race. A thunderstorm raged outside, but there was a storm raging in Speed's heart as well.

The Masked Racer told me not to enter the Trans-Country Race, Speed thought. A clap of thunder boomed loudly outside. *Who does he think he is? I think he's afraid I'll beat him. There's only one way to prove that I can. I've got to enter that race.*

Lightning lit up Speed's room, charging the air with electricity.

Pops says I need more experience, Speed thought. *Well, I'll go to the track now and I'll get experience!*

Speed got out of bed and quickly got dressed. His mom and dad were asleep, so he tiptoed quietly to the door that led to the garage.

Speed heard a noise behind him. Heart pounding, he turned. Then he sighed in relief. It

was only Spritle, sleepwalking in his pajamas.

In the garage, Speed put on his racing helmet.
He climbed into the Mach 5. Then he opened the
electric garage door.

A ferocious wind blew in through the open
door, knocking everything off of the shelves.
Outside, the rain hammered down.

Speed revved the Mach 5's engine. He knew
what he was doing was foolish, but he didn't
care. He wanted to race. That was all he had ever
dreamed of. He had to prove to Pops that he could
follow his dream.

Speed drove into the pouring rain.

Speed could only see a few yards in front of him as he drove to the racetrack. That didn't slow him down. He hugged every turn on the highway. Soon he smelled salt in the air, and the round stadium of the racetrack loomed in front of him.

Speed roared down the track. Through the rain, he saw headlights in front of him, then a flash of yellow. He wasn't alone.

Speed stepped on the brakes. He got out of the Mach 5.

Crack! Lightning bathed the track in bright white light.

The yellow car stopped in front of Speed. Racer X got out and faced him.

"You!" Racer X cried. "What are you doing here, Speed?"

"Practicing," Speed said, his voice cold.

"You can't enter that race, Speed," the Masked Racer said firmly.

"I can beat you," Speed said. "I'll prove it."

Speed jumped back into the Mach 5 and sped away.

"Wait!" Racer X called out. He climbed into his car and took off after Speed.

What had started as practice had now become a race. The two cars zoomed down the track. Then they left the track and drove onto the slick highway. Speed was in the lead, but just barely.

The road took a steep drop down a hill and then straightened out through a mountain pass.

The rain pounded even harder now, and Speed could barely see in front of him. But anger and determination pushed him on, and he recklessly picked up speed. One wrong turn could send the Mach 5 crashing into the rocks.

The road widened. Racer X came up quickly on Speed's left side and passed him. Speed frowned. He gritted his teeth and stepped on the gas, pushing the limits of the Mach 5. He charged ahead, speeding past Racer X.

Then the mountain road took a sharp turn. Speed skidded, maneuvering the turn on his two right wheels. Sparks shot out from his tires.

Speed struggled to get control of the car. But a

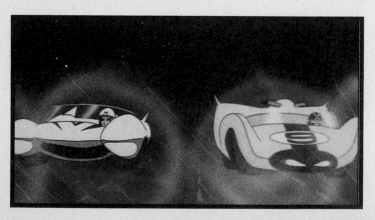

pile of fallen boulders blocked the road up ahead. Speed didn't have time to steer around them.

He quickly hit the A button on his steering wheel. The hydraulic lifts sent the Mach 5 flying over the boulders. But when the tires hit the wet road, Speed couldn't get enough traction to make a safe landing. The Mach 5 hit a rock and went into a spin!

Speed's stomach lurched as the Mach 5 spun into one 360-degree turn after another. He pressed the B button on the steering wheel. Ridged coverings surrounded the tires, giving Speed the traction he needed. He straightened out the car.

Speed still couldn't get the Mach 5 to ride

smoothly. He struggled to control the steering wheel as the car banged into the metal guardrail. He heard a sickening screech as the side of the Mach 5 scraped against the railing.

Now the mountain road followed the ocean coast. Angry waves slapped against the barrier wall to the left of the Mach 5. To his right were the jagged rocks of the mountain.

Racer X tried to catch up to Speed. He expertly steered through the fallen boulders. A jagged bolt of lightning struck the mountain, blinding him for a moment. Worried, the Masked Racer turned on his radio.

"The forecast for the day of the big race is still

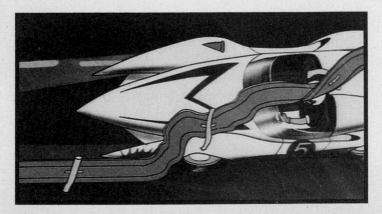

uncertain," said the radio announcer. "Right now we're in the center of a low-pressure area that is bringing heavy rains and high winds. At sea the waves are thirty feet high and the tide is still rising. Driving conditions are extremely hazardous. Stay off the roads tonight."

Racer X frowned and turned off the radio. He knew firsthand that the announcer was right. The high waves were pouring over the guardrail, making the road even more slick and dangerous.

Over in the Mach 5, water splashed up onto the windshield, making it impossible for Speed to see. He gasped. He veered onto the side of the road, and barreled into a bunch of oil drums. *Bam! Bam! Bam!* The metal drums smacked into the Mach 5 and bounced off of the road.

"Speed!" Racer X cried.

Speed quickly regained control of the car, but only for a moment. The storm raged more violently now, and Speed lurched back and forth across the road. He struggled to straighten out.

I won't give up and stop the car, Speed told himself. *I've got to show Racer X what I can do. I've got to keep driving!*

To his left, a boat was thrashed about by the powerful waves. The boat crashed into the retaining wall, sending chunks of concrete flying toward the Mach 5.

Speed turned the steering wheel sharply to avoid crashing into the debris himself. But his trouble wasn't over. An avalanche of logs came tumbling down the mountainside.

"Ahhhh!" screamed Speed as he braced himself.

The Mach 5 was about to crash!

The logs tumbled across the road. There was nowhere to steer, no time to jump. Speed stepped on the brakes as hard as he could.

Wham! The Mach 5 crashed into the logs.

Speed's world went black. His car door flew open, and his limp body fell out of the race car.

Racer X stopped his car in time. He walked out into the rain and picked up Speed's body. He carried Speed to his car. Then he radioed a service station and had them tow the Mach 5 back to the racetrack.

A few hours later, the rain had stopped. Speed was sleeping peacefully on a spare bed in Racer X's house. He wasn't hurt, but he hadn't opened his eyes once since the crash.

Racer X hovered over Speed, a concerned look on his face. Stormy thoughts filled his mind.

It's true that in every race I enter there are terrible crashes, Racer X thought. *But people are wrong to think that I caused them. I am not an evil man. Someone is out to get me. I don't know who it is. But every time I race, my mysterious enemy puts other racers in danger. That's why I don't want you in the Trans-Country Race, Speed. I don't want you to get hurt. There is a good reason. I want to protect you.*

Racer X closed his eyes as he thought of a day years ago, the day of his own first race. He opened his eyes and looked at Speed.

"You see, Speed, I am secretly your older brother, Rex Racer," he said softly. "Years ago, when I had no experience in racing, I took the

special racing car that Pops had built and I entered the top race at the Sunny Downs Track. I wanted to win more than anything. I wanted to be world's champion."

Racer X remembered the roar of the car's engine, the feeling of pure energy that flowed through him as he raced around the track. For the first time in his life, he had felt truly alive.

Within seconds, that feeling changed to pure terror.

"I lost control of the car and crashed," Racer X remembered. It all seemed like a bad dream now. "I was lucky to be alive, but I still wanted to race again. Pops was furious at me. It wasn't just because I had wrecked his car. He was angry that I had raced without the experience and skill I needed to be a good driver. He told me I couldn't race again. I argued with him, but he refused to change his mind."

Racer X shook his head, remembering. The argument had been furious. Pops was always so stubborn. Racer X had stormed off, filled with a determination to race—with or without Pops's approval.

"Finally, I had no choice," Racer X continued.

"I decided to go away to learn, to practice, and to compete until I could become the world's champion race car driver. I vowed that no one would learn my identity until I achieved that goal. Until I do become the world champion, Speed, nobody will ever learn that I am really Rex Racer, your older brother. Not even you, Speed."

Racer X turned and left the room.

Speed slept on. He had no idea that he had been saved by his long lost brother.

And if Racer X had his way, Speed might never know.

The next morning, Trixie drove her yellow convertible around town, looking for Speed. Spritle and Chim Chim sat in the backseat. Spritle was busy licking a vanilla ice-cream cone.

"I wonder where he could be," Trixie said, frowning. "It's not like Speed to disappear like this. I certainly hope nothing has happened to him."

Spritle looked up at Trixie while she was talking. Chim Chim saw his chance and quickly gulped down Spritle's ice cream.

"It's strange, but the Mach 5 has disappeared, too," Trixie remarked.

Spritle turned back to his ice cream. All that was left was the cone!

He leaned over the seat, giving Trixie his sweetest smile.

"I told you about the letter I gave him from the Masked Racer, so buy me some more ice cream!" Spritle said.

Trixie shook her head. "You've eaten so much, I may have to buy you some tummy medicine!"

Trixie switched on her CB radio. Speed was always tuned to the same channel. She could usually reach him on the CB.

"Come in, Speed," Trixie tried. "Speed, are you there?"

The only response was the static from the radio. Trixie was starting to really worry. She didn't know what that letter from Racer X had said, but something told her it had something to do with Speed's disappearance.

"I guess we'd better check with the Masked Racer himself," Trixie reasoned. It was a good thing the news crews had followed the mysterious racer to his home last night. She knew just where to go.

Spritle grinned. "I'm glad I told you, Trixie. I know we'll find Speed!"

Speed opened his eyes. Sunlight streamed into the room.

"Where am I?" Speed asked groggily. "I don't remember a thing."

Speed sat up. He was in bed, wearing a bathrobe over his clothes. He looked around the room. The modern-looking apartment was filled with racing trophies, photos of race cars, and books about racing. Curious, Speed climbed out of bed.

A table against the wall held a vase filled with

white roses. Speed walked to them and sniffed the flowers.

White roses, Speed mused. *These are Mom's favorite flowers.*

Then something caught Speed's eye. There was a white racing uniform draped over an orange armchair in the room. Next to the uniform was a black mask.

Speed picked up the mask. He gasped.

"This belongs to the Masked Racer!" he cried.

The events of the night before came flooding back to Speed. The logs had come tumbling down the mountain . . . the Mach 5 had slammed into them . . .

Racer X must have saved me, Speed realized. *He's brought me to his house.*

Speed could hear the patter of water in a shower in the next room. The Masked Racer was in there . . . without his mask.

"Now I can find out who he is," Speed said.

Speed looked at the mask in his hands. He was filled with curiosity. What was it like to be the Masked Racer? He put the mask over his face.

For a second, Speed imagined what it would be like to be behind the wheels of a race car. To race without anyone knowing who you were . . .

The Masked Racer's identity was a real mystery. But Speed had a rare chance to learn the truth. With the mask still on, he tiptoed toward the shower door.

Creeeeak.

Speed heard a noise behind him. Startled, he turned around. A man wearing a trenchcoat, hat, and sunglasses stood there. Before Speed could cry out, the man raised his arm . . .

Bam! Speed didn't know what hit him. He fell to the floor, groaning.

Another man in a trenchcoat appeared. Speed was out cold. They carried him outside and shoved him in the backseat of a white convertible car, where two more thugs waited.

"We got Racer X!" one of the men announced.

Of course, the criminals didn't know it, but the man they had captured wasn't the Masked Racer. It was Speed, wearing Racer X's mask!

The two kidnappers climbed into the front seat and revved the engine. Just then, Trixie pulled up.

Spritle pointed to the man he thought was Racer X in the car.

"There's the Masked Racer!" he yelled.

Trixie got out of the car and walked over to the white convertible.

"Have you seen Speed Racer?" she asked.

"Sorry, girlie, but we haven't seen him," said

the first man. "So long!"

Trixie frowned. Why was the Masked Racer ignoring her on purpose? And what was he doing with these rude men, anyway?

"I thought he might be with the Masked Racer," Trixie said hopefully.

"Well, he's not!" the thug snapped. Then he sped away.

Trixie was annoyed. "The Masked Racer pretends to be asleep. What kind of man would do that?"

She turned back to her yellow car and saw that backseat was now empty.

"Now where did Spritle and Chim Chim disappear to?" she wondered.

An alarming thought crossed her mind. She quickly looked back at the white convertible as it headed down the road. Spritle and Chim Chim peeked out of the trunk. Then they shut it.

"Oh, no!" Trixie cried. Those two were always getting into trouble. *They must have been suspicious of the Masked Racer and his friends,* Trixie guessed. *But why?*

She sighed and ran to her car. It was bad enough that Speed was missing. Now she had to chase after Spritle and Chim Chim!

Up ahead, the white car turned off of the road into the woods. There was a click, and a new license plate slid down over the car's original license plate. Then one of the men got out of the car and began to peel away at the white covering on the car. It wasn't white paint at all, but a clever disguise! Underneath, the car was a bright red.

The man jumped back in the car, and the driver brought the car back on the road. Trixie was

just catching up. She blinked when she saw the red car.

"That's strange," Trixie said. The car she'd been chasing was white. Had she lost it?

While Trixie puzzled over this, the red car took a turn down another wooded road. It stopped in front of a fancy-looking house. The goons dragged Speed inside and tied him to a chair. Two thugs stood on either side of Speed. Spritle and Chim Chim watched the scene through a window.

A short, fat man in a suit stepped in front of the room. It was Mr. Wiley, the secret owner of the Alpha Team!

"Welcome, Masked Racer, to my humble mansion," Wiley said, grinning like a snake. "Make yourself comfortable. You'll be staying here until the Trans-Country Race is over."

Speed was just starting to wake up. He quickly figured out what was happening. Wiley wanted the Masked Racer out of the race for some reason. He thought Speed was the Masked Racer. That's

why he had been kidnapped and tied up.

Better keep my mouth shut, Speed told himself. *I'll make my move when the time comes.*

"You think you're so clever, keeping your identity secret," Wiley bellowed. He poked Speed with his walking stick. "Your secret is over now, Masked Racer. I'm about to find out who you really are."

Wiley nodded to the thugs. "Remove the mask!" he demanded.

"Yes, sir!" said one of the men.

He pulled off the mask, revealing Speed's face.

"What!" Wiley sputtered.

"It's my brother!" Spritle cried from the window.

Speed pushed off the ropes and threw the bathrobe to the ground.

The thug next to Speed looked angry. "You put on the Masked Racer's mask to make fools of us, huh?"

"You're wrong," Speed shot back. "I was trying on the mask when somebody sneaked up behind me and hit me. It's not my fault that you made a mistake."

Speed glared at his captors. "It makes sense to me now. Everyone thinks the Masked Racer causes crashes in his races. But he's innocent. You and your men are sabotaging him, aren't you?"

Wiley laughed. "Don't get excited, kid. That's none of your business."

"So don't waste your time trying to find out the truth!" the thug added.

Outside the window, Spritle looked worried.

"We'd better find Trixie!" he said.

He turned to run—and bumped right into Mr. Fixer, Wiley's right-hand man! The thin man

grabbed Spritle and Chim Chim by the straps of their red overalls. Then he carried them inside the house.

"I caught these two snooping outside," Fixer told the men.

"Spritle!" Speed cried.

"How come you let these men take you here, Speed?" Spritle asked. "Don't you know they are part of the Alpha Team?"

Speed was startled. "What?"

"I recognize this guy," Spritle said, nodding up toward Fixer. "He's the same man who offered

Pops a bunch of money for you to join the Alpha Team for the big race."

Speed turned to Wiley. "So that's why you tried to capture the Masked Racer!" he realized. "You're afraid he'll be able to beat your team."

"It's too bad you've discovered my plans for the Trans-Country Race," Wiley said darkly.

Before Speed could react, Wiley's four thugs lunged forward and grabbed Speed. He tried to break away, but the four musclemen had him in a tight grip.

Speed couldn't get away, but Chim Chim had

other ideas. He swung up and bit Mr. Fixer in the arm!

"Ow!" Mr. Fixer yelled.

He let go of his grip on Chim Chim. The little chimpanzee ran out of the door as fast as he could. Then he jumped up to the nearest tree. He used his powerful arms to swing from tree to tree.

Fixer started to give chase, but Mr. Wiley stopped him.

"Let him get away," Wiley said, chuckling. "Monkeys can't talk."

Then he nodded to his thugs. "Take Speed Racer to the cellar and tie him up. Make sure the ropes are tight this time," he said. "Bring the kid, too."

Speed's blue eyes burned with anger as the thugs ushered him and Spritle downstairs. It hurt him to see Spritle's scared face.

Don't worry, Spritle, Speed promised silently. *I'll get us out of here.*

Chim Chim soon reached the highway and jumped down to the road. He was good at swinging on trees, but he needed a faster way to get to Trixie. Luckily, a farm truck came rumbling past. He jumped onto the back of the truck and perched on top of a hay bale.

But the truck wasn't going fast enough for Chim Chim. He leaped off the truck onto the roof of a blue sports car. Wind whipped through his fur as the car tore down the road. That was more like it!

Chim Chim kept an eye out for Trixie. He didn't have to wait long. Up ahead, he saw Trixie's yellow car at a gas station.

The blue car came to a stop at a traffic light. Chim Chim tumbled off of the roof and onto the hood of the car. The startled driver screamed.

Chim Chim didn't have time to apologize. He ran up to Trixie. She was talking to the station attendant.

"It was a big, white convertible—I mean a big, red convertible," she was saying. "Anyway, it was a convertible and it changed color. I didn't know it was the same car until I stopped following it. Did you see it?"

The attendant scratched his head. He had no idea what Trixie was talking about.

Chim Chim tugged on Trixie's skirt. She looked down and gasped.

"Where did you come from? And where's Spritle?" she asked.

Chim Chim jumped on the trunk of Trixie's car. He began to jump up and down, waving his arms.

"What are you saying, Chim Chim?" Trixie asked. "Are you trying to tell me that Speed and Spritle are in trouble? And that you'll show me where they are?"

Chim Chim nodded. The attendant shook his head. These were the strangest customers he'd had all day!

Trixie jumped into her car. "Let's go!" she told Chim Chim. He jumped in the car behind her.

Trixie pealed out of the gas station and hurried down the road.

She had to help Speed and Spritle!

Speed looked around the basement of Wiley's mansion. The dark, damp space was filled with oil drums and old gas cans. The only light came from a flickering gas-powered lantern perched on a rickety shelf.

He tried to stay calm. The men had tied ropes around his waist and arms. They'd done the same to Spritle, too. One thug had been left in the basement to guard both of them. Speed could

probably run if he had the chance. But he couldn't leave Spritle behind.

I've got to figure out a way to get out of here, Speed thought. *I've got to warn everybody about the plans these crooks have to win the Trans-Country Race.*

Then the sound of a police siren pierced the air.

"The police are coming!" Spritle cried.

"Huh?" The nervous thug turned to look. Speed saw his chance.

Bam! Speed jumped up and kicked the oil drum the goon was sitting on. The surprised man fell to the floor.

"Come on, Spritle!" Speed yelled. His little brother jumped up and ran after Speed.

"I'll get you!" the thug roared as he scrambled to get to his feet. But he slipped in the oil pouring from the drum and fell once more.

As Speed and Spritle tried to escape, the oil drum rolled across the floor and knocked over the rickety shelf. The gas lantern toppled over, onto the floor.

"Hurry!" Speed urged Spritle. They charged up the stairs. Fear made Speed run faster than he'd ever run before. Once the flames from the lamp hit the spilled oil—

BOOM! The fiery explosion rocked the basement. The flames burst through the floor of the mansion and then began to spread throughout Wiley's house.

Trixie and Chim Chim pulled up right when the explosion hit. She screamed in horror.

"Speed! Spritle!"

She ran toward the house. If they were in there, Trixie had to save them. Chim Chim followed behind her. A searing heat hit her face as she neared the front of the house. Then she heard a mighty groan as one of the front walls toppled forward.

A strong hand pulled her back just in time. Trixie turned to see the Masked Racer.

"Racer X!" Trixie cried.

"Stay here, Trixie," the Masked Racer said calmly. "I'll go after Spritle and Speed!"

Racer X bravely ran into the burning house.

The orange flames grew stronger and higher with each moment. Trixie held her breath. What if the Masked Racer couldn't find them in time?

But Racer X ran out seconds later. He carried Spritle in his arms, and Speed rested on his left shoulder. He brought them away from the house and laid them on the ground.

Down below, they saw a car drive down the road, away from the mansion. The car held Wiley, Fixer, and the rest of the thugs. They had all escaped the flames.

"Thanks for saving our lives, Masked Racer,"

Speed said gratefully. "Those goons from the Alpha Team tried to capture you so you wouldn't be able to compete in the Trans-Country Race. But they got me instead."

"I've come across them before. They'll stop at nothing to win," the Masked Racer told them.

Trixie felt angry. Those men had done more than try to fix a race—they'd almost killed Speed and Spritle!

"They're a bunch of criminals," she said firmly. "We should tell the police about them."

"Don't worry. I'll be able to handle them," Racer X replied. "But I don't think you can, Speed. This race is going to be dangerous. I want you to keep out of it."

The Masked Racer began to walk away.

A mix of emotions flooded through Speed. The Masked Racer had saved his life twice already. But that didn't give him any right to tell Speed not to race!

"I've got to be in the race!" Speed protested.

The Masked Racer stopped. "Take my advice, Speed. You'd be foolish to enter this race."

He climbed into his race car without another word. Speed and Trixie watched him drive off.

"What are you going to do, Speed?" Trixie asked.

Speed got to his feet. He felt a little shaky, but not hurt. He knew what he had to do.

"My mind's made up, Trixie," he said. "I don't care what Pops says. Or Racer X. I'm going to race!"

Crowds of racing fans filled the stands at the racetrack. The smell of peanuts and popcorn filled the air, as well as an electric current of excitement. The Trans-Country Race was about to begin!

Trixie stood on the side of the track, along with Speed's friend and mechanic, Sparky. Some not-so-friendly people were in the crowd, too— Mr. Wiley and his henchman, Mr. Fixer.

Four trumpeters in red uniforms stood on the track. They played a lively fanfare announcing

the start of the race. The tune blared from the stadium's loudspeakers.

High above the stadium, a television announcer watched the scene from a clear booth. Cameras stationed along the track would capture the race from every angle for fans watching at home.

"The great Trans-Country Race is about to get underway, with racers competing from almost every country," the announcer said. "Thirty six of the fastest cars in the world are competing. They're lined up and ready to go. There are over one hundred thousand fans here, tensely

waiting for the start of the most important race of the year."

Pops and Mom Racer were in their living room, watching the cars line up on their TV screen.

"I know Speed wanted to see the race," Mom said. "I wonder where he is. Do you know?"

"I'm afraid to find out," Pops grumbled. "You know Speed. He's always up to something."

They settled down to watch the race.

"The Masked Racer is nowhere in sight. This race may start without him," the announcer continued. "That means that the number one contender in this race is newcomer Speed Racer, driving the Mach 5!"

"Did I hear right?" Mom asked. "Did that announcer just say that Speed's going to be in the race?"

"You heard right," Pops replied. He held his breath, trying not to explode. How dare Speed disobey him!

"Aren't you angry?" Mom asked.

"Who, me? Angry?" Pops said innocently. He didn't want to give his feelings away. He had to find some way to stop Speed—and he didn't want Mrs. Racer to talk him out of it.

A red race car with a number 2 on it drove up to the starting line.

"Driving for the Alpha Team in car number 2 is Mr. Zoomer Slick," the announcer said.

Mr. Fixer walked up to Slick.

"Now remember, no matter what, you've got to win," he warned menacingly.

Slick looked confident. "I'll beat 'em all!"

Speed drove up to the starting line in the

Mach 5. Mr. Wiley watched him from the stands, fuming.

"Speed Racer!" he said. "I thought that fire took care of him."

Mr. Fixer casually leaned on Wiley's seat. He didn't look worried at all.

"We'll take care of Speed yet," Fixer promised. "Just watch."

Speed hunched over the steering wheel of the Mach 5, fiercely concentrating.

"The race begins in three minutes!" the announcer cried. "Start your engines!"

Speed revved the engine of the Mach 5. The

sound of the rumbling motor was his favorite sound in the world. It was the only sound he heard. Everything else—the screaming fans, the music, the other cars—faded into the background.

"There's one good thing," Fixer told Mr. Wiley. "It looks like the Masked Racer is too chicken to be in the race. We must have scared him off."

Back at the Racer house, Pops tiptoed to the front door.

"Where are you going?" Mom asked.

Pops stopped. "For a walk around the block," he said innocently.

"Well, I'd like to go out, too," Moms said. "So I guess you won't mind taking me—to the track!" She laughed.

Pops and Mom Racer headed to the track. In the meantime, the race was about to start. A small, plump man in a blue suit stood on a platform next to the starting line. He had a small yellow flag in his hand.

"The head of the racetrack association will

signal the start of the Trans-Country Race by lowering the flag," the announcer said.

As soon as the little man lowered the yellow flag, all thirty-six cars tore down the track at lightning speed.

Speed started off at the head of the pack. He could see Zoomer Slick not far behind him. The rest of the Alpha Team drove red race cars like Zoomer's. He knew he'd have to watch out for them, too. He had to win this. He had to prove to Pops and Racer X that he could really race!

The race announcer's voice came over Speed's radio. He sounded excited.

"Hey! What's this? One more car is entering. I'm unable to make out its number yet."

The crowd gasped. Thousands of heads turned to the startling line to see the mysterious late entry. As the car sped closer, everyone could see it was bright yellow, with a number 9 on the side.

"Ladies and gentlemen, it's the Masked Racer!"

The crowd turned ugly. Instead of cheering, they booed.

"We don't want him!"

"He'll cause too many crashes!"

Mr. Wiley was unhappiest of all. "I don't want the Masked Racer winning this race!" he fumed.

"Don't worry," Fixer assured him. "I have the perfect plan to take care of him."

Mr. Wiley grinned. "Excellent!"

The Masked Racer may have had a late start, but he sped to the head of the pack quickly. Soon he was just yards behind Speed.

"Look, Sparky, the Masked Racer is going to catch up to Speed!" Trixie cried.

"Speed'll keep his lead," Sparky said.

Speed drove the Mach 5 past Trixie and Sparky. Sparky held up a sign with a number 4 on it.

"It's the fourth lap, Speed!" Sparky called out.

Speed looked in the rearview mirror and saw the Masked Racer gaining on him. Speed tried to go faster, but the Masked Racer caught up, like a sleek jungle cat closing in on its prey.

"Speed, I warned you!" Racer X called out. "Get out of the race while you still can! There's

going to be a lot of trouble here."

Speed just ignored him. He had come too far. He wasn't going to give up now.

Each time the cars zoomed around the track, Speed grew more confident. Everything was going smoothly. He was staying in the lead—but he had competition.

"We're now in the twentieth lap of the great Trans-Country Race, and the leading cars are still the Mach 5, driven by Speed Racer, the Masked Racer's car, and the Alpha Team's car," the announcer reported. "The rest are following close behind. All cars will be pulling into the pit soon for refueling and quick repairs."

Mr. Fixer nudged Mr. Wiley. "That's what I've been waiting for. When the Masked Racer comes in for refueling, the pit crew will fill up his radiator with gasoline instead of water!"

"The radiator?" Wiley asked.

Mr. Fixer nodded. "Just wait till he starts up . . ."

"He'll go bang!" Wiley said, understanding. "Brilliant!" He looked through a pair of binoculars

at the pit crew. "Good job. I see our boys waiting."

Two men in yellow jumpsuits waited in the pit for the Masked Racer. They looked like normal mechanics, but they were really Wiley's thugs.

Things looked grim for the Masked Racer. Luckily, two tiny heroes were hiding nearby. They'd heard every word of the evil plan.

Spritle turned to Chim Chim. "Did you hear that? We've got to go. We've got to save the Masked Racer!"

Spritle and Chim Chim ran off through the crowd. They had to get to the pit stop before the Masked Racer got there! Spritle darted between the legs of the race fans in the crowd. Chim Chim jumped on their heads. They jumped over the wall separating the fans from the track and ran to the pit stop.

The two goons stood next to a tank marked "F" for fuel. They were watching the track, waiting for Racer X to pull up.

Spritle and Chim Chim worked fast. They wheeled the tank away and replaced it with a water tank. Wiley's thugs didn't even notice.

The Masked Racer squealed into the pit stop. The thugs ran over, wheeling the tank.

"We got the water for your radiator," one of the thugs said.

They opened the hood and began to fill the radiator with a hose. Wiley watched the scene through his binoculars, laughing. He had no idea he'd been tricked.

The men finished the job. Racer X zoomed back onto the track. Wiley and the thugs watched, waiting for the Masked Racer's car to explode.

It didn't. Racer X sped safely down the track. Spritle and Chim Chim cheered from the stands.

Wiley and Fixer exchanged confused glances.

"Go to plan B," Wiley ordered.

Fixer waved his hat in the air, sending a signal to Zoomer Slick.

Slam! Just as planned, Slick crashed into the car on purpose. The force of the crash loosened Racer X's left rear tire. The Masked Racer spun out of control, nearly crashing into the guardrail. But he quickly regained control and avoided the crash.

The tire went spiraling down the track just as one of the other members of the Alpha Team approached. Driver 3 yelled out as the rolling tire came toward him. The driver sharply spun his steering wheel to avoid the tire, but he lost control of the car.

Wham! He collided into the guardrail, crushing the front of his car like an accordion. The driver

wailed and shook his fist. He was out of the race!

But Fixer's tricks weren't done yet. One of the thugs sat in the stands. He used a mirror to reflect the bright rays of sunlight right into the Masked Racer's eyes!

When the Masked Racer turned his head to avoid the glare, it gave another one of the Alpha Team's drivers the chance to sneak up on the Masked Racer's right.

Slam! The driver crashed into the Masked Racer. Racer X spun out, struggling to gain control of the car.

Then the mirror trick backfired. The glare blinded the Alpha Team driver. He lost control of his car and plowed into the guardrail. Just as the car burst into flames, the frightened driver ran to safety.

Now Racer X's car was skidding down the track on its two right wheels. It was headed right for Alpha Team car 1. The driver couldn't steer out of the way in time, and flew over Racer X's car. It landed with a sickening crash. All four wheels exploded from the impact.

Back in the mechanics' pit, Spritle and Chim Chim watched the race with Pops and Mom Racer.

Spritle watched through binoculars. The track was a mess of twisted metal, but Speed was way ahead of all the trouble. Most of his competition had been wiped out.

"Yay, Speed!" Spritle cheered.

Pops grabbed the binoculars from Spritle.

"Come on, Speed!" he yelled. "You can win this!"

Speed raced past Sparky. This time, instead of a lap number, Sparky had drawn a picture of Pops on the card. Speed got the message—Pops was at the track.

But nothing, not even Pops, could break Speed's concentration now. There were only a few

more laps to go, and he still had the lead. Zoomer Slick was behind him on the left, and the Masked Racer was trailing behind, doing his best with only three tires.

Suddenly, the picture changed. Two more members of the Alpha Team seemed to come out of nowhere. Cars 4 and 5 crept up on either side of Speed and then quickly moved in front of him. They weaved back and forth, making it impossible for Speed to get ahead.

Without warning, car 4 pulled back.

Bam! Car 4 slammed Speed from behind.

Bam! At the same time, car 5 backed up, slamming the Mach 5 in the nose.

The double blow sent the Mach 5 spinning out of control. Speed steered hard, trying to get the car back on track.

There was nothing he could do. The Mach 5 was about to crash into the guardrail!

Racer X zoomed in between Speed and the guardrail. His car prevented the Mach 5 from crashing, but the Masked Racer wasn't so lucky. He skidded along the curved guardrail like a skateboarder on a half-pipe. Then his car flipped over, landing in the middle of the track. Another race car steered to avoid the Masked Racer and collided right into Alpha Team car 4. The red car flew up in the air and slammed back down onto the track, bursting into flames.

Racer X banged into the flaming car, and his own race car went spinning out of control again. The yellow car stopped against the concrete wall.

Speed saw the crash in his rearview mirror. He quickly stepped on the brakes and turned, whipping into a 180.

Racer X had saved him three times now. It was time for him to help Racer X.

"It's the last lap of the race but Speed is going back to the scene of the accident!" the announcer cried in disbelief.

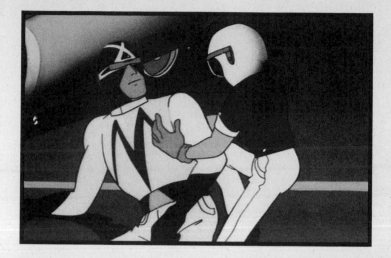

The brakes squealed as Speed stopped the Mach 5. He jumped out and ran to the Masked Racer. Racer X climbed out of the car, groaning and clutching his arm.

"You shouldn't have stopped racing because of me," he told Speed. "I'll be all right. Go on. Get back into your car."

"You saved my life!" Speed said. "I'm not going to leave you. You need my help!"

"We're in the middle of a big race," Racer X reminded him. "This isn't the time for personal feelings, Speed. Get back into your car. I'm going

to get back into mine. It can still run, and I'll do my best to win."

With a pained look on his face, Racer X pulled himself onto his feet, clutching the side of his race car.

"I'm going to beat you, Speed," he promised.

Speed knew there was nothing he could do. He climbed back into the Mach 5. He stepped on the gas.

If Masked Racer wanted to race, then he would race!

The crowd of fans could barely wait to see what happened next.

"This is the last lap," the announcer said. "Alpha Team car 2 has a huge lead, thanks to all the accidents we've seen today. The Masked Racer is pushing his car to the side, where he'll try to make some repairs. It looks like Zoomer Slick is going to win this race!"

Racer X quickly worked to repair his car. Speed focused on the red car ahead of him.

Zoomer Slick had been playing dirty all day. Now it was time to teach him a lesson, fair and square.

The crowd roared with excitement as they watched Speed come up from behind.

"Here comes Speed Racer!" the announcer cried. "He's back at the wheel of the Mach 5. He's coming up fast."

"Go, Speed, go, go!" Trixie cheered, jumping up and down.

The announcer looked amazed. "And now the Masked Racer is back in the race!"

Speed and Slick were racing side by side. Racer X came up right between them, catching up with amazing speed. The racing official stood at the finish line, holding the black-and-white checkered flag. From his point of view, all three cars were neck and neck.

Speed braced himself for the final push of the race. He had to win. He had something to prove— to Pops, to the Masked Racer, and to himself.

Speed stepped on the gas.

The last seconds of the race were super fast, but they felt like slow motion to Speed.

He surged forward, willing the Mach 5 to move ahead with every cell in his body. The push was just what he needed. He roared past the finish line, and the checkered flag dropped.

"Speed Racer is the winner!" the announcer yelled. "The Masked Racer takes second place!"

Speed couldn't believe it. He slowed the Mach 5 to a stop. He had done it!

"Yay, Speed!" Trixie, Sparky, and Spritle cheered and waved. Chim Chim did a victory somersault.

In the stands, Mr. Wiley growled and waved his cane. It accidentally bonked Mr. Fixer on the head.

Speed waved to the cheering crowd. Confetti rained down on his head. Winning was a really amazing feeling!

Pops cheered from the sidelines. "Hooray! I always knew you'd be able to do it, Speed."

Mom Racer gave him a questioning look. Pops remembered he was supposed to be angry

at Speed. He frowned and shook his fist in the air.

"You disobeyed my orders!"

Mom Racer laughed. "Speed did a wonderful job and we're both very proud of him, right?"

Pops sighed. He hated to admit it, but Mom Racer was right. He was proud of Speed. He and Mrs. Racer walked up to Speed's car. Trixie, Sparky, Spritle, and Chim Chim were gathered around Speed.

"Wasn't he just great?" Sparky asked Pops. "Wasn't he just great? Why don't you let him be a racer and drive the Mach 5 all of the time? You know he'll have a good chance of winning. He'll take good care of the Mach 5, too."

Trixie looked at Pops with wide eyes. "Please, sir. Please let Speed be a professional racer. Please?"

Pops didn't answer for a moment. Then he smiled at Speed.

"You can be a racer," he said.

Speed gasped in surprise. Spritle cheered, and Chim Chim did a flip. But Speed was so stunned, he couldn't say a word.

Sparky patted Speed's racing helmet.

"Hey, isn't that just great?" Sparky said.

Sparky lifted Speed onto his shoulders. He carried Speed toward the judges' table. Trixie ran by his side, and Spritle rode on Chim Chim's shoulders.

"Hooray for Speed! Hooray for Speed!" they cheered.

The Masked Racer watched the scene from a distance. His heart was heavy. He had been part of that happy family once. But he had made a vow to never contact them until he was world champion, and he wasn't going to break it.

The racing judges waited beside the trophy table for Speed.

"Hey, there are the judges," Speed told his friends. "Cut it out! We've got to look professional."

Speed gazed at the big trophy he was about to receive. He should have been thrilled, but he had mixed emotions. Winning was incredible—but his victory was bittersweet. If Racer X hadn't saved him, Speed wouldn't even have finished.

The Masked Racer is the real winner, a real champion, Speed thought. *I saw for myself how skillfully he can drive. He's a far better driver than anybody. He's a far better driver than I am.*

Speed jumped off of Sparky's shoulders and ran toward the parking lot, leaving the trophy behind on the table.

"Hey, where are you going?" Sparky called out.

Speed didn't answer him. He had to find the Masked Racer. But there was no sign of the yellow car anywhere.

"The Masked Racer is gone," Speed said softly. "I wanted to ask him why he let me win."

But Racer X was only hiding. He watched his little brother scan the parking lot.

"Speed, I hope you'll be the best racer in the world," he whispered.

Racer X jumped into his car and drove away. Speed caught a glimpse of the Masked Racer as he drove away.

"Someday, I'll find out who he is," he vowed. "Someday, the two of us will race each other, one on one."

Speed walked back to the stadium. He had a trophy to accept.

Racer X drove off into the sunset.

That late-night practice race I had against Racer X is one I'll never forget. Driving in the dark is always an extra challenge. Throw in pounding rain, powerful winds, and dangerous lightning and you've got a recipe for disaster. It was nearly impossible to keep ahold of the Mach 5 on the slick, wet road. And the ocean waves spilling over the rail just made everything worse.

That wet and wild race reminds me of another one-on-one race I had with pro racer Kim Jugger. And in this race, there wasn't a drop of water in sight!

It all started when I decided to enter the Desert Race in the country of Sandoland. Great racers from around the world were traveling to this far-off country to compete. I was at the airport with Trixie and Sparky, waiting for the Mach 5 to be loaded onto the plane.

Then a race car drove up onto the runway and slammed into the Mach 5! The car was called the Black Tiger and it belonged to Kim Jugger, a champion driver. I couldn't believe he'd crashed into the Mach 5. He was really arrogant—he said he thought the Mach 5 was supposed to be a superior car and could take the damage. Then he ordered the men to load the Black Tiger onto the plane first! I was really steamed at that guy.

Trixie, Sparky, and I boarded the plane. We didn't know it, but Sprite and Chim Chim had come on board, disguised as a little girl and a baby. They were almost discovered, so they hid in the cargo hold of the plane. There, Sprite saw a mysterious, one-eyed man put a package inside the Black Tiger.

When we landed in Sandoland, Kim's car got unloaded first. Before our eyes, it exploded into flames! Kim examined the car and found Sprite's slingshot in the backseat. He blamed Sprite for sabotaging the car. Kim actually thought I put Sprite up to it!

Kim and I almost got into a fight. Sparky helped me cool down. I had to focus on the Desert Race.

But after Kim left, Spritle told me about the one-eyed man. I knew I had to tell Kim what had happened. I found out that Kim had gone home to Flathill Country of Sandoland. So Trixie and I climbed into the Mach 5 and rode out into the barren desert to find Kim.

That's how our desert adventure started. Want to find out how it ends? Then strap on your seat belt, slather on some sunscreen, and get ready to read about this exciting bonus race!

CHASE ACROSS THE SAND

The morning sun was just rising over Sandoland, but already waves of heat were rising up from the sand. The Mach 5 forged ahead into the desert.

Speed was on a mission. He had to find Kim Jugger. He wanted to tell him what had really happened to his race car, the Black Tiger. Sure, Kim hadn't been very nice to Speed. But Speed hated to see one of his fellow drivers in trouble.

Speed gazed around the desert as they drove.

Orange sand stretched across the land for miles and miles. There were no buildings or trees in sight, only jagged hills of sand. It felt like the middle of nowhere.

As they rode, a hot wind began to whip up around them. The wind picked up the sand until the air all around them became an orange cloud.

"I can hardly see in this sandstorm!" Speed exclaimed. He pressed the D button on the steering wheel of the Mach 5. A clear pod came over the cockpit, sealing it from the elements. Then he carefully drove the car to the base of the hill, where they were somewhat protected from the winds.

The sandstorm dumped piles of sand around the Mach 5's wheels. When it finally ended, Speed opened the cockpit.

The trunk of the Mach 5 opened, too. Sprite and Chim Chim popped their heads out—they had stowed away, as usual.

"This is the biggest sandbox I've ever seen!" Spritle exclaimed.

But Speed and Trixie didn't notice the stowaways just yet. An army of men appeared on the hillside. The men rode camels and wore blue uniforms. Yellow scarves protected their heads from the sand and sun.

The camel riders charged at the Mach 5. Speed quickly got the car in gear. He jammed the gas pedal, but the wheels spun uselessly in the sand. Speed tried again. He had to get the Mach 5 moving!

Finally, the wheels got traction. Speed roared out of the sand and zoomed across the desert floor. The camels followed behind him. Speed was amazed. The beasts were almost as fast as his race car!

They drove over a hill, only to see another army of men on camels charging toward them.

"Oh, no!" Trixie cried.

Speed quickly turned left to avoid them. Both

armies converged, racing behind Speed. Speed frowned. He couldn't get enough of a lead on them. The camels were too fast, and the Mach 5 was sluggish on the desert sand.

In the trunk, Spritle and Chim Chim went to work.

"It's time we counterattack, Chim Chim," Spritle said.

Chim Chim nodded. He handed Spritle a small rock. Spritle put the rock in his slingshot, then let it go.

Whack! Spritle knocked one of the riders right off of his camel!

Whack! Whack! Spritle had great aim. Riders were falling left and right.

Speed saw the action in his rearview mirror.

"We've got help of some kind coming from the trunk," he noticed. He quickly realized what had happened. Spritle and Chim Chim had stowed away again!

But Spritle's help wasn't enough. The Mach 5 roared to the top of a hill. Speed saw a steep drop below. He hit the A button on the steering wheel to activate the hydraulic jacks. Instead of crash-landing, the Mach 5 hopped across the desert floor. It landed in front of a tall fortress made of stone and sand.

When the race car came to a stop, the men surrounded them. Their leader came forward.

"What are you doing here?" he demanded.

"We're headed for Flathill Country, to find Kim Jugger," Speed explained.

The man raised a black eyebrow in interest.

"I see. Then I have news for you. We are an army of rebels from Flathill Country," he said. "You are wanted as a spy. You must come to our fortress!"

CAPTURED BY REBELS

The rebels led Speed, Trixie, Spritle, and Chim Chim to the steps of the fortress. Speed knew he couldn't fight a whole army of rebels by himself. He'd have to wait to see what was in store.

The loud bang of a gong signaled that something important was going to happen. A man in a yellow uniform and a white cape stepped out of the fortress. A bearded man with a patch over one eye stood behind him.

Speed gasped. It was Kim Jugger—and the man behind him must be the man Spritle had seen sabotage the Black Tiger!

"Kim, you're a member of the rebels?" Speed asked.

"My father is commander of all of the rebels

from Flathill Country," Kim said. "I think it's brave of you to travel all this way, Speed, but I still think you're a coward for what you did to my car. I will have my men throw you in jail!"

"I didn't do it!" Speed protested. "I can point out the person who destroyed your car. He's the man standing right behind you!"

The one-eyed man grimaced.

"My brother Spritle saw him put something in your car on the plane," Speed explained.

The one-eyed man stepped forward. "What

are you waiting for? You heard Kim's order. Throw them in jail!"

Two rebels stepped up and grabbed Speed and Trixie by the arms.

"First, burn the Mach 5!" the one-eyed man ordered. "Burn it!"

Speed watched, helpless, as the rebels aimed flamethrowers at the Mach 5.

Was this the end of the greatest racing car in the world?

THE RULES ARE SET

Speed couldn't stand by and watch the men destroy the Mach 5. He jabbed the man holding his arms with his elbows. The man groaned and let go.

Speed jumped with all his might. He tackled the nearest rebel to the ground, wrestling the flamethrower from his hands.

Speed jumped back to his feet as another rebel

came toward him. Speed easily picked him up and flipped him, throwing him into the sand.

The one-eyed man charged down the steps. His good eye burned with anger.

Before he could attack, a loud voice stopped him.

"Enough!"

A tall man in uniform stood on the steps of the rebel fort. The one-eyed man stopped in his tracks. The rebels lowered their flamethrowers. Speed looked at the Mach 5. Miraculously, it wasn't damaged.

"I am General Jugger, leader of the rebels," he said. "What Speed Racer said is true. I ordered my cousin, Ben Schemer, to destroy the Black Tiger. I did it to keep my son out of the Desert Race."

"Father!" Kim cried. "Why did you destroy my chances to enter the race?"

The general looked downcast. "I wanted your help here, at the fort," he said.

"Kim, now you know I wasn't lying," Speed said.

"Yes, but it's too bad about my car," Kim said. "Now I won't be able to enter the race."

"You would have lost, anyway," Speed said angrily. He didn't usually taunt his competitors, but Kim had almost thrown him in jail and tried to burn up the Mach 5. He wasn't feeling very nice.

Ben Schemer stepped forward. "There is only one way to know if the Black Tiger can beat the Mach 5," he said. "The two of you must race! I'll get the Black Tiger repaired right away."

"You can repair most of it, but the special brake system can never be replaced," Kim said sadly.

"Then I have a solution," Schemer said. "To make you both equal, the Mach 5 won't have any brakes, either."

Kim looked at Speed. "Will you race without brakes?" he asked.

Speed hesitated. No brakes? That was more dangerous than anything he'd ever done before.

But a chance to race Kim Jugger was just what he was itching for. He could finally put their feud to rest. And a race across the sand would be good practice for the big Desert Race coming up.

"I'll do it!" Speed said.

Ben Schemer grinned. "Excellent!" he said. "The race will begin tomorrow morning. You will race around the Palace of Doom!"

A TRAP!

Speed and Kim were up the next morning before the sun. By the time the sun peeked over the horizon, both drivers sat in their cars, engines humming. The Black Tiger had been fixed, just as Ben Schemer had been promised. Speed felt comfortable behind the wheel of the Mach 5— and glad that it hadn't been burned to a crisp!

A soldier gave Speed a small cloth bag.

"The race will be many hours long," he said. "This food will sustain you."

"Thanks!" Speed said. He put the bag on the seat next to him. The man gave a bag of food to Kim, too.

One of the rebels shot a gun to start the race. Speed and Kim took off toward the rising sun.

"Be careful and good luck!" Trixie called.

"Do your best to win!" Spritle cheered.

"Eeek!" Chim Chim added.

Ben Schemer watched the drivers until they were specks in the distance.

"This is the last race for them both," he said darkly. He nodded toward Trixie, Spritle, and Chim

Chim. "Make them all prisoners!" he ordered the soldiers.

The soldiers grabbed Trixie, Spritle, and Chim Chim. Then they grabbed the general, too!

"I am the commander of the rebel army now," Schemer said.

Trixie and the general were helpless to stop them. Spritle, however, got lucky.

As a soldier carried Spritle toward the jail cells, Chim Chim jumped on the soldier's back, knocking him to the ground. Spritle and Chim Chim jumped on a camel. The frightened beast reared its head, then began to run away.

"We've got to help Speed!" Spritle cried.

SUN, SAND, AND SCORPIONS

Speed and Kim had no idea that Ben Schemer had taken over the rebel army. They both focused on the race. The sun burned down mercilessly on them, but Speed's desire to win burned hotter.

I've got to beat Kim, Speed told himself. Sweat poured down his face, nearly blinding him. *I can't give up!*

Speed was so focused on the road that he didn't notice the bag on the seat next to him was moving. It didn't contain delicious food. Each bag contained a deadly scorpion! No doubt Ben Schemer was responsible.

Without Speed noticing, the creature climbed out of the bag and headed for Speed's arm . . .

In the Black Tiger, the other scorpion had gotten loose, too. It climbed up Kim's boot, then onto his knee.

"Ah!" Kim cried. He looked over at the Mach 5. The scorpion had climbed up Speed's shirt! It clung to his shoulder, just seconds away from Speed's face.

"There's a scorpion on you!" Kim called out over the roar of the engines.

Speed glanced down and saw the creature on his shoulder. He cried out in alarm. He felt the scorpion's sharp little legs as it crawled onto his helmet.

"I've got one on me, too!" Kim yelled. "Get ready to jump out of your car. I'll jump at the same time. We'd better start slowing down."

Speed held his breath. One wrong move, and the scorpion might lash out and sting him with its poison-tipped tail. But he couldn't stop the car without brakes. Kim was right. Jumping was the only solution.

Speed took his foot off of the gas. The Mach 5 slowed down to a crawl. Speed carefully unhooked his seat belt and slowly opened his door.

"Jump!" Kim cried.

Speed hurled himself out of the Mach 5 onto the sand. He rolled and rolled down a hill. The scorpion went flying off of him, then skittered away.

Speed got to his feet and dusted the sand off of his clothes. Kim was doing the same. The Mach 5 and the Black Tiger had slowed to a complete stop up ahead.

"If we'd been stung, that would have been the end," Kim said.

"They were planted in our cars," Speed said with certainty.

"When we get back, I'll investigate," Kim told him. "But right now, we need to get back to the race. I'm going to beat you!"

"Oh, yeah?" Speed's blue eyes glittered at the challenge. He and Kim were racers at heart. It would take more than a bunch of bugs to stop this race.

Speed and Kim ran to their cars. They revved their engines at the same time, then sped out over the sand.

QUICKSAND!

Speed and Kim raced along the desert. The bright yellow sun seemed to take up the whole sky. Speed had never been hotter in his life. And he'd never wanted to beat anyone more than he wanted to beat Kim.

Suddenly, another sandstorm kicked up. Speed closed his cockpit and braced himself against the strong winds. Kim surged ahead, gaining the lead.

Then, right before Speed's eyes, the swirling sands swallowed the Black Tiger whole!

Speed stopped the Mach 5 and ran out of his car. He looked down into a pit of spinning sand. Kim stood on top of the Black Tiger's hood. His car was slowly sinking.

"Speed!" Kim called out. "I'm stuck in quicksand!"

Speed daringly slid down into the pit. He grabbed Kim's arm, then pulled with all his might.

"We're almost out!" Speed cried.

He gave a mighty pull, and Kim climbed up out of the pit with him. They reached the edge, then both drivers jumped into the Mach 5.

Speed stepped on the gas, but the wheels spun round and round. Speed had parked too close to the quicksand! He could feel the pull of the quicksand on the race car. Then, a sudden, strong force pulled the Mach 5 under the sand!

At that very moment, an army of men appeared on the hilltop. They wore white uniforms and rode camels.

The men shot grappling hooks into the sand, attached to cables. The leader of the men cried, "Haul!" As a unit, they began to pull the Mach 5 out of the pit.

Speed lowered the top of the cockpit, and he and Kim coughed and sputtered as they breathed the fresh air once more. They had been rescued! But who had saved them?

ANOTHER DARING RESCUE

The truth became clear to Speed when he saw Spritle and Chim Chim on the hilltop. Spritle told Speed everything—how Ben Schemer had taken over the rebel army and imprisoned Trixie and Kim's father. How they had escaped on a camel. How they were lost in the desert when the government army found them and saved them.

But their desert adventure was not over yet. The government army led a charge against the rebel fort, led by Speed in the Mach 5. They rescued Trixie and the general—just in time for the Desert Race.

Kim couldn't race, because his Black Tiger was lost in the desert forever. Speed would never know if he could beat Kim—but that didn't seem so important now. All that mattered was that Trixie, Spritle, and Chim Chim were safe.

Speed looked around the racetrack, with its concrete walls and bright lights. It seemed like a piece of cake, compared to the brutal Desert Race he'd just run.

The starting gun sounded. Speed grinned and stepped on the gas.

Now that the danger was over, he could concentrate on what he liked best about racing—having fun!

SPEED RACER
THE NEXT GENERATION™

**Racing to DVD
May 2008**

*Classic Speed Racer DVDs
Also Available!*